SHERLOCK GNOMES

JULIET SAVES THE DAY!

Adapted by A. E. Dingee
Illustrated by Kelly Kennedy and Scott Burroughs

Ready-to-Read

Simon Spotlight
New York   London   Toronto   Sydney   New Delhi

SIMON SPOTLIGHT
An imprint of Simon & Schuster Children's Publishing Division
1230 Avenue of the Americas, New York, New York 10020
This Simon Spotlight edition February 2018
TM & © 2018 Paramount Pictures. All Rights Reserved.
SIMON SPOTLIGHT, READY-TO-READ, and colophon are registered trademarks of Simon & Schuster, Inc.
For information about special discounts for bulk purchases, please contact Simon & Schuster Special Sales
at 1-866-506-1949 or business@simonandschuster.com.
Manufactured in the United States of America 1217 LAK
10 9 8 7 6 5 4 3 2 1
ISBN 978-1-5344-1095-4 (hc)
ISBN 978-1-5344-1094-7 (pbk)
ISBN 978-1-5344-1096-1 (eBook)

Oh no!
Gnomeo and Juliet's new home
in London was a complete mess.
And all their friends and family
were missing!

Luckily, Sherlock Gnomes,
a great detective, agreed to take
the case.
His friend Dr. Watson
was there to help too.
Watson always helped collect clues.

Sometimes Sherlock was rude
to people. Watson tried
to smooth things over for his friend.
Sherlock knew who was behind
the missing gnomes.
He was certain his enemy,
Moriarty, had taken the gnomes.

Juliet and Gnomeo wanted to help
find the missing gnomes.
They followed Sherlock and
Dr. Watson underground
and into the sewers.

They kept cranky cats away
while Sherlock searched for clues
in a shop.

They used paper lanterns
to parachute onto
a moving bus.

Then they jumped from
the bus to a tree.
They got lucky.
No humans spotted them.

Gnomeo wanted answers.
"All right, smart guy. What's your
plan?" he asked Sherlock Gnomes.
But Sherlock would not share
his plan. He would not listen
to Gnomeo.

Gnomeo set off on his own.
Watson knew how Gnomeo felt.
He told Juliet, "Don't worry.
I'll get him back."
Juliet stayed to help Sherlock.

They spent the night in a museum.
Juliet waited while Sherlock
considered the clues.
They wore a squirrel costume and
went to a park.
They found the next clue there.
It was a button.

Sherlock followed the new clue
to Irene—his former girlfriend!

But Irene refused to help.
Instead she sang a song.

Then she had her friend Big Ted
toss her visitors out the door.

Juliet was fed up.
She banged on Irene's door.
"You've got something I need,
and I'm not leaving without it!"
she yelled.

Irene let Juliet back inside.
"I don't care about Sherlock!
He's the most annoying gnome
I've ever met!" said Juliet.
She told Irene all about Gnomeo.
Juliet impressed Irene.
So she gave the new clue to Juliet.

Finally Juliet had the last
piece of the puzzle. It was
a message for Sherlock.
And it was marked
with another *M*!

"You already know
it's all about you,
so what is the pattern
in the final clue?"
read Juliet.

Sherlock thought about the clues.
He put them together in his mind.
The clues started to fit together.
They formed the shape of a place
Sherlock knew well.
It was called Traitor's Gate.

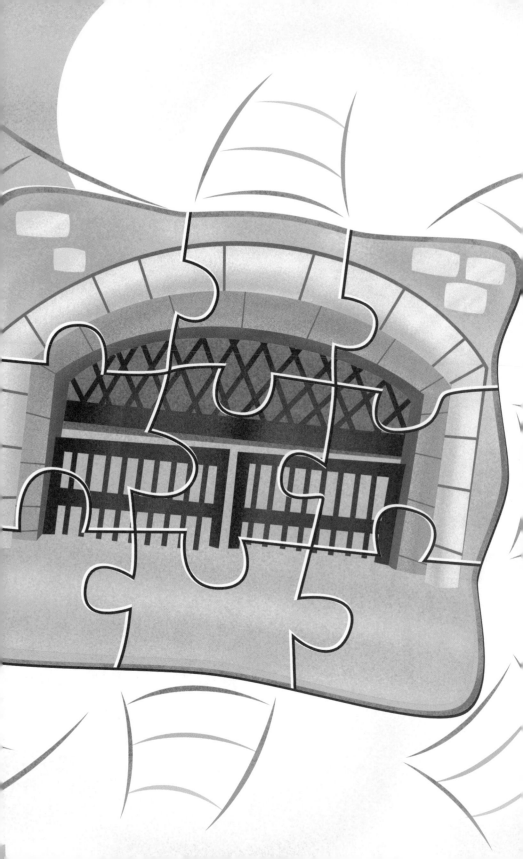

Traitor's Gate was the water gate
for the Tower of London.
It was where Sherlock and Watson
had solved their first case!
He and Juliet had to get
to the tower fast.
But the tower was miles away!

The subway was the only way
to make it there in time.
They jumped onto the bumper
and held on tight!

The train twisted and turned
on the tracks.
Sherlock slipped off.
He grabbed the bumper.
Then Juliet grabbed him.
She saved Sherlock!

Sherlock and Juliet
survived the subway ride.
They made it to Traitor's Gate
just in time to face off
with the kidnapper.

"Show yourself!"
Sherlock shouted.

While Sherlock faced off
against the kidnapper,
Juliet sprang into action.
She spotted a drone nearby.
Juliet took the controls
and flew toward the bridge.

Gnomeo had been kidnapped
and was being held at the bridge.
Juliet saved him just in time.

Thanks to Juliet,
Sherlock solved the case.
The case was closed.

And thanks to Juliet,
Gnomeo and the gnomes
were safe.
It was time to celebrate
in the Purple Garden.
Sherlock, Watson, and even Irene
came to the party.

Hooray!
The gnomes cheered
for Juliet and her Gnomeo.